PIRATE BABY

Story by **Mary Hoffman**

Pictures by **Ros Asquith**

Otter-Barry BOOKS

The pirate ship, *Ramshackle,* was sailing lazily between islands when the lookout spotted a strange object floating on the water.

"**Something Ahoy!**" shouted the lookout, whose name was Ben, peering through his telescope.

Strange object

The first mate, Barnacle Barney, steered the *Ramshackle* towards the object. "It's a ... it's a ... well, shiver me timbers," said the captain, Jolly Roger. "It's a baby!"

He was quite right.
And soon all the pirates could hear it.

The baby was bawling at the top of its lungs. It was on a little raft no bigger than the lid of a barrel, woven from twigs and branches, and it was soon going to roll over the edge.

The *Ramshackle* reached it
just in time and the bosun,
Red Bart,
swarmed
down
the side
of the
boat and
snatched up
the howling
red-faced baby.

"Poor little chap," said the ship's cook, Spoons McGill. "He's hungry."

"What can we feed him?" asked Captain Jolly Roger. "We don't have a cow."

"Hang on," said Spoons and went below. He came back with a tin of condensed milk. He made two holes in the lid, poured some milk into a cup and then added fresh water from a barrel.

But the baby did not know how to drink from a cup.

It kept on howling.

"Emergency measures!" said Captain Jolly Roger. **"Fetch the doctor."**

Up came the ship's doctor, Crossbones, with a syringe and filled it with milk. He squirted some into the baby's mouth until it stopped howling and fell asleep in the captain's arms.

"What are we going to do about the other end?"
asked Barnacle Barney.

"Leave it to me," said Crossbones,
brandishing a flag and some scissors.

The baby's nappy was **so stinky**
they dropped it over the side.
But they kept the pin.

What a surprise – it was a **girl** baby!

"'Tis unlucky to have a woman aboard ship," said Barney.

"Hardly a woman," said Crossbones. "I'm not a baby doctor, but I'd say she was about four months old."

"And as for unlucky," said the captain, "how lucky she was that we came along! She was bound for Davy Jones's Locker."

At the next island they came to,
the islanders were so scared to see
a pirate ship that they gave them
a nanny-goat to make
milk for the baby.

HELP! Pirates!

"We should have asked for gold and jewels," grumbled Red Bart as they sailed away.

"The baby can't eat those," said Spoons.

The baby became very fond of the goat and soon said *"Nananana"* when she was hungry. So they called the goat Nana and the baby Isla, because they found her near an island.

There was a ship's cat called Plunderpuss and a noisy parrot called McSquawk. Isla loved them.

She loves ME the best.

And she loved all the pirates who looked after her — but she loved the captain, Jolly Roger, best of all.

Spoons the cook got out his sewing machine and made her a stack of nappies, which they took turns to wash in a bucket.
He made her some clothes out of old pirate vests.

NAPPIES AHOY!

PIRATE PATTERNS by HOOK & AYE

And Red Bart the bosun made her a toy squid out of an old pair of gloves.

It was her **best** thing — after the goat and the captain.

Months went by and Isla learned to crawl on the deck.

Barney, who had forgotten about females being unlucky on a boat, made a barrier out of old fishing nets so that she wouldn't fall overboard.

Not THAT kind of NET!

"We aren't doing much pirating," said Red Bart one day.

"'Twouldn't be a good example to little Isla," said the captain.

"Bah!" said Barney — we're just getting soft."

"All right. The very next ship we see," said the captain, **"we'll board 'em and plunder 'em!"**

But the next ship they saw was full of
women pirates!

"Do you think we ought to ask them to take Isla?" asked Crossbones, clutching the baby to him.

"Certainly not!" said the captain. "Avast ye, Barney, and full speed ahead."

Soon the women pirates were out of sight and the crew of the *Ramshackle* relaxed.

Then. . .

SWOOSH!

Out of the deep came
a sea-monster.

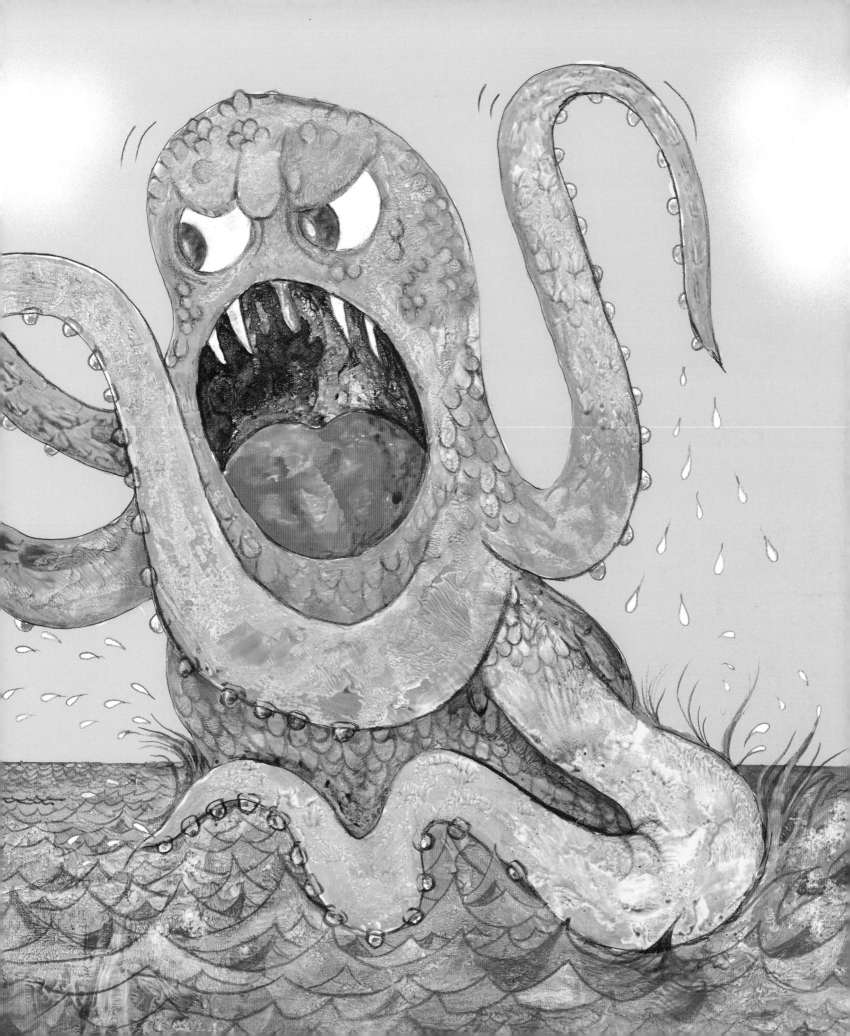

It towered over the ship.
"Quid!" cooed Isla, as all
the pirates tried to hide.

"The *Ramshackle*'s a goner!"
whispered Red Bart.
"It'll sink us for sure.
Someone rescue the baby."

But the monster looked
at the baby and stretched out
a long tentacle full of suckers.

"Oh no you don't!" said Jolly Roger.
"You can't have our baby."
And he drew his cutlass.

But little Isla held out
her toy squid to the monster.

And the monster took it and carried it off
to the deep to be his very own —
he just wanted something to play with.

"Isla saved the *Ramshackle* from
the monster," cheered the crew.
"She is a true Pirate Baby!"

And so she was!

Isla lived happily with the pirates
until she grew up to be a famous pirate herself.
But that's another story.

For my grandchildren, Rocket and Indigo, the boat babies — MH

For my great nephew Theo — RA

Text copyright © Mary Hoffman 2017
Illustrations copyright © Ros Asquith 2017
The right of Mary Hoffman and Ros Asquith to be identified as the author
and illustrator of this work has been asserted by them in accordance with
the Copyright, Designs and Patents Act, 1988 (United Kingdom).

First published in Great Britain and in the USA in 2017 by
Otter-Barry Books, Little Orchard, Burley Gate, Herefordshire, HR1 3QS

www.otterbarrybooks.com

A catalogue record for this book is available from the British Library.

ISBN 978-1-91095-995-4

Illustrated with watercolour and photoshop

Printed in China

9 8 7 6 5 4 3 2 1